SpongeBob SquarePants

Hands OFF!

by David Lewman

illustrated by C.H. Greenblatt and William Reiss

SIMON SPOTLIGHT

New York   London   Toronto   Sydney   Singapore

Stephen Hillenburg

Based on the TV series *SpongeBob SquarePants*® created by Stephen Hillenburg as seen on Nickelodeon®

SIMON SPOTLIGHT
An imprint of Simon & Schuster Children's Publishing Division
1230 Avenue of the Americas, New York, New York 10020

Manufactured in the United States of America
First Edition
10 9 8 7 6 5 4 3 2 1
ISBN 0-689-85603-2

SpongeBob was playing with his best friend, Patrick. He slid down Patrick's rock, sprinted over to Squidward's house, and ran up the side.

"Beat that!" yelled SpongeBob happily. "That's my fastest time yet!"

"Oh, yeah?" shouted Patrick. "I bet I can do it even slower! I mean—faster!"

Squidward leaned out of his window. "Will you two be quiet?!" he said, snarling. "I'm trying to practice my clarinet!"

"But, Squidward, we're playing a really fun game," Patrick explained. "See, you slide down my rock, then you zip over to your house, and run up the side—"

"I *know* what you're doing," said Squidward, interrupting. "Just stop it! You're being too loud!"

"Why don't you play with us, Squidward?" asked SpongeBob. "It's fun!"

Squidward noticed the mailman pulling up to SpongeBob's house.

"Why look, SpongeBob," he said, pointing. "Isn't that the mailman at your house? It looks like he's carrying a box. . . ."

"A box!" shouted SpongeBob. "That's just what I've been waiting for!"

To:
SpongeBob
SquarePants

This Side Up

MAIL

SpongeBob carefully opened the box. "At last," he whispered. "Do you realize what this is, Patrick?"

Patrick nodded. "I have no idea," he said slowly.

SpongeBob trembled with excitement. "This," he explained, "is a genuine Mermaid Man and Barnacle Boy Bubble Blower . . . in its original packaging!"

Command the Creatures of the Deep!

Made in the China Sea

MERMAID MAN AND BARNACLE BOY

BUBBLE

"Wow," said Patrick. "What does that mean?"
SpongeBob gently lifted the Bubble Blower and stared at it.
"I've been trying to find one of these for years. Isn't it great?"

Patrick jumped up and down with excitement. "I love Mermaid Man and Barnacle Boy! Come on, SpongeBob—let's blow some bubbles! I'll bet they'll be the best bubbles in the whole world!"

SpongeBob looked shocked. "Blow some bubbles? But, Patrick, we can't open this. We have to leave it in the original packaging."

Patrick scratched his head. "Why? What good is a toy if you can't play with it?"

SpongeBob smiled. "Oh, Patrick," he said. "This isn't just a toy. It's a *collectible* toy. It's for collecting—not playing."

Patrick was still confused. "But then what do you do with it?"

"Lock it in a closet," explained SpongeBob. "Or maybe, on special occasions, display it on a shelf."

Patrick stared at the Bubble Blower. "Can I put it on *my* shelf, SpongeBob?" he asked.

"Patrick," said SpongeBob, "you don't have a shelf."

"I could *build* one," said Patrick. "Then I could look at the Blubble Bower—"

"Bubble Blower," corrected SpongeBob.

"—as I fall asleep," continued Patrick. "Please?" he pleaded. "Just for one night? I'll be your best friend."

"You already *are* my best friend," said SpongeBob. Then SpongeBob thought hard. He decided that best friends share all their things—even their favorite things. "All right, you can borrow the Bubble Blower for one night," he said.

"Hooray!" yelled Patrick as he grabbed the package and ran off.

SpongeBob shouted after him, "Remember—don't open it!"

At nighttime SpongeBob got ready for bed. "Good night, Gary!" he said. "I sure am glad I let Patrick borrow my new Bubble Blower. That's what best friends do."

"Meow," said Gary.

"I'm sure he'll be extra careful with it," said SpongeBob. He patted Gary and climbed into bed.

But as he lay in bed SpongeBob started to worry about all the things Patrick might be doing with the Bubble Blower. Had he taken it out of the package? Was he using up all the soap bubbles? Or was he doing something really terrible, like breaking the Mermaid Man bubble wand?

SpongeBob couldn't take it anymore.
He got up, put on his clothes, and went
downstairs. Gary followed him.

"Sorry, Gary," SpongeBob said. "I'm not
taking you for a walk. I'm just going to sneak over to Patrick's house and make
sure everything's okay with my new Bubble Blower."

Gary frowned.

"And don't give me that look," said SpongeBob.

SpongeBob creeped past Squidward's house. As he tiptoed up to Patrick's rock he thought about his precious Bubble Blower. "Please be in the box. . . . Please be in the box. . . . Please be in the box," he thought aloud.

SpongeBob entered Patrick's house as quietly as he could. Patrick was asleep and snoring loudly.

SpongeBob spotted the Bubble Blower on Patrick's new shelf. It was fine! Patrick hadn't broken it! He hadn't even opened it!

"I should have trusted him," said SpongeBob.

"See you in the morning, pal," whispered SpongeBob very quietly. But as
he turned to go he tripped over a shell and fell with a loud crash!

Patrick sat up in bed, wide awake. "SpongeBob!" he yelled. "What are you
doing here?"

"I'm sorry, Patrick," said SpongeBob, embarrassed. "I was just . . . um . . . well, I guess I was just a teensy bit worried about my Mermaid Man and Barnacle Boy Bubble Blower."

Patrick quickly put on his shorts. He was shocked. "You mean you didn't trust me? Your *best friend?* That's terrible! I can't believe it!"

Patrick was so upset that he started waving his arms and jumping up and down. He started knocking things over, sending his things crashing to the ground.

"My own best friend! Not trusting me!" he yelled. "I would never, ever break anything of yours! What do you think I am—careless?"

"Patrick, please!" called SpongeBob. "You're breaking all your stuff!"

Patrick stopped and looked around at all the things he'd broken. "Gee, SpongeBob. I guess I *am* a little bit careless," he said. "You were right to be worried. You'd better take your Bubble Blower home before I break it."

Patrick walked over toward the Bubble Blower, tripped, and almost knocked it off the shelf! "*You* pick it up!" he cried. "I shouldn't even touch it! I'm just a big, clumsy oaf!"

SpongeBob picked up the Bubble Blower and
started to walk out of the house.
But then he stopped and turned around.
"Come on, Patrick!" he yelled. "Follow me!"
Patrick quickly followed.

BUBBLE BLOWER

Outside, SpongeBob began to take the packaging off the Bubble Blower.

"SpongeBob!" yelled Patrick. "What are you doing?"

"What good is a Bubble Blower if you can't blow bubbles with it?" asked SpongeBob. "Wanna play with it?"

"I sure do!" said Patrick.

SpongeBob dipped the wand into the bubble liquid and handed it to Patrick. "Here, Patrick," he said. "You can blow the first bubble."

"Wow," said Patrick, as his eyes widened. "The first blubble . . . I mean, bubble."

Patrick blew a big bubble, and then SpongeBob blew one, and they continued to blow bubbles into the wee hours of the morning.

Squidward didn't get much sleep that night.